My Great Big Mamma

Olivier Ka
Pictures by Luc Melanson

Translated by Helen Mixter

Groundwood Books House of Anansi Press Toronto Berkeley

My mamma is big. Very big. She is the biggest mother in the world.

When she comes into my room, she takes up all the space. She leans to the left, she leans to the right, she leans over me. She's the only thing I can see.

Her hands are pillows, her arms are bolsters. And her chest... as soon as I lay my head on her chest, I feel like falling asleep with a great big smile on my face.

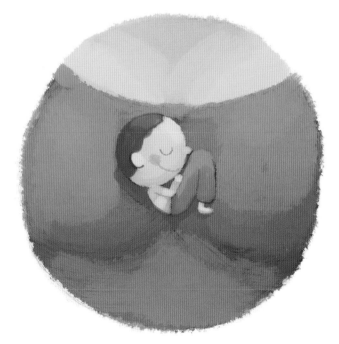

My mamma gives me noisy kisses.
They go "shmops" on my cheek.
That tickles me. Her kisses mean,
"I love you so much, I want to eat
you right up."

I wouldn't even mind if she did eat me up.

Sometimes when we are walking down the street together, children point their fingers. They say to their mothers, "Look how fat that woman is."

That makes me proud. If my mamma wanted to, she could pick up twenty kids at a time. But I'm the only one who gets to enjoy her.

My mamma takes up two seats on the bus, but because I sit on her lap, we only take up the normal amount of space. Except for one thing. I'm more comfortable than anyone else. If all the bus seats were as comfortable as my mamma, well then, people wouldn't be so grouchy.

When my mamma laughs, her whole body laughs, too. It's a laugh quake.

But one day, not long ago, Mamma said,
"I have to lose weight. I'm going on a diet."

A diet?

After that she began to pay attention to what she ate. She didn't enjoy eating anymore, you could tell. She looked sad when she saw what was on her plate.

No wonder. A little serving like that? That's not right for a big mother. It's like giving a tiny little bone to a huge dog. How silly.

I asked her, "Why do you want to lose weight?"

"So I'll look prettier," she answered.

That's crazy. She wouldn't be prettier. She'd be thinner, that's all. And less cuddly, and less soft.

I could already imagine myself with a skinny little mother. No chest, no tummy, arms like sticks. I'd be afraid of breaking her.

To show her how stupid it is to go on a diet, I decided to go on a diet, too.

No more salads because they make you slimy like a snail.

No more potatoes because your brain might turn into mashed potatoes.

No more hamburgers because you could become a cow.

No more yogurt because it's too white and erases all the other colors.

My mamma asked me why I was being so fussy about my food. I told her that I was on a diet, just like her. She laughed. But it wasn't funny.

She said, "You don't need to lose weight. You are perfect just the way you are."

I answered, "So are you. You are the
most beautiful mamma in the world."

She gave me a great big kiss and then she gave up her diet. She started eating lots again, and she got her smile back. Meals became a feast once more.

I said to her, "I like it better when you aren't on a diet."

She answered, "Me, too. You know I only did it because of other people."

Other people? What do other people have to do with it?

Everything about my mamma is big –
her body, how much she loves to eat, her
love. I want her to stay that way.

And I always want to be able to fall
asleep in her soft arms. Because in there,
it's so nice and safe that nothing bad
can ever happen to me.